Freddie
as F.R.O.7.

Jon Acevski and David Ashton

WARNER BOOKS

Freddie as FRO7
A Warner Book

First published in Great Britain in 1992 by Warner Books

Copyright © Hollywood Road Film Productions Limited 1992

The moral right of the authors has been asserted.

Design by Between The Lines
Illustrated by HRFP Artists
Adaptation by Belinda Hollyer

A CIP catalogue record for this book is available from the British Library.

ISBN (HB) 0 356 20112 0   ISBN (PB) 0 356 20113 9

Printed by Graphicom SRL, Italy

Warner Books
A Division of Little, Brown and Company (UK) Limited
165 Great Dover Street
London SE1 4YA

PRINCE FREDERIC

Once upon a time, in the country of France, there was a prince called Frederic, who was ten years old. His mother, the Queen, had been mysteriously drowned at sea the year before, so his father, the great Magician King, was a sad and lonely man.

He and Frederic spent hours together, and Frederic tried to cheer his father's spirits with magic tricks, while his father tried to teach his son all that he knew. Frederic was his father's heir, and one day he would rule the kingdom in his father's place. He had a lot to learn – and with time, patience and hard work, Frederic would be as great and good a king as his father.

But the King's sister, Messina, had other plans. Messina also had magic powers, but hers were as black as the night, and she was as wicked as the King was good. She despised her brother and hated Frederic, and she plotted against both of them, and watched and waited for a chance to overthrow the King. Then only Frederic would stand between Messina and her ambition to rule the kingdom. Once she had dealt with the little prince, all the power would be hers alone!

So Messina bided her time while she perfected her evil plans and practised her venomous spells. Finally, Messina was ready to strike.

Frederic sensed her evil presence watching as he and the King mounted their horses and left the palace to go hunting. He shivered in fear. Something was very wrong, he knew it.

The forest seemed to have fallen silent, as though even the wild creatures were holding their breath. Frederic wished that he was powerful enough to protect his father from danger.

But it was too late. Just at that moment, a huge snake appeared from nowhere, as if by magic, hissing and slithering around the King's horse. The horse reared in fear – and the King was thrown over the cliff, down to the rocks below. He was killed instantly.

The whole kingdom mourned the death of their king, for he had been greatly loved. Only Frederic suspected that Messina had arranged her own brother's death, so the nobles who came to the funeral decided that Messina should rule the kingdom, until Frederic was old enough to become king.

Poor Frederic! He sobbed bitterly on his father's coffin, until Messina herself led him away. Her face did not betray her secret triumph. At last! Frederic was in her power!

Messina took Frederic to her tower room, and locked all the doors. Then, turning to a magic mirror on the wall, Messina began to cast one of her wicked spells – the spell that had helped her to destroy her brother; the spell she believed would help destroy his son. As Frederic watched, frozen in horror, Messina's body shivered in a mist that writhed and pulsed, and formed into a huge and terrible snake – the very snake that had frightened his father's horse!

And then, as the snake turned and slithered towards Frederic, its cruel mouth opened wide – and Messina's wicked laughter echoed around the tower! With Frederic destroyed, Messina's power would be complete. Again and again, Messina struck at Frederic, and at first the young boy managed to avoid her. But the snake's dark powers were immense. She changed her shape again, launching a bolt of magic lightning, which descended mercilessly on to the terrified boy. When the mist cleared, Frederic was no longer a young boy. His wicked aunt had

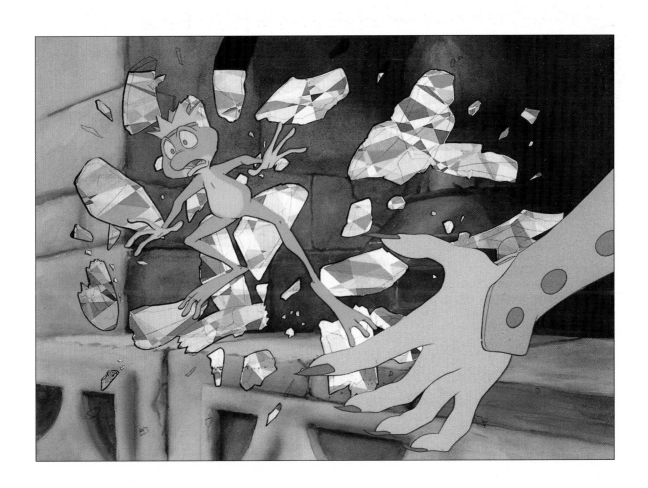

succeeded in turning him into a frog! Now she could capture him, and do whatever she wanted! Frederic did not fully understand what had happened to him, but he knew he must try to escape. Only the open window seemed to offer hope, and the little frog–prince managed to clamber on to the sill, and peer down. How far it was to the water! But Frederic had no time to waste, for Messina was coming towards him with an upside-down plant pot in her hands. Too late he suddenly realised that a tiny frog could easily be captured in such a trap. His evil aunt crashed the pot down over him so hard that it smashed into a thousand pieces. Frederic jumped – down, down, down – into the sea far below. Furious, Messina leaped after him, changing into a snake once more.

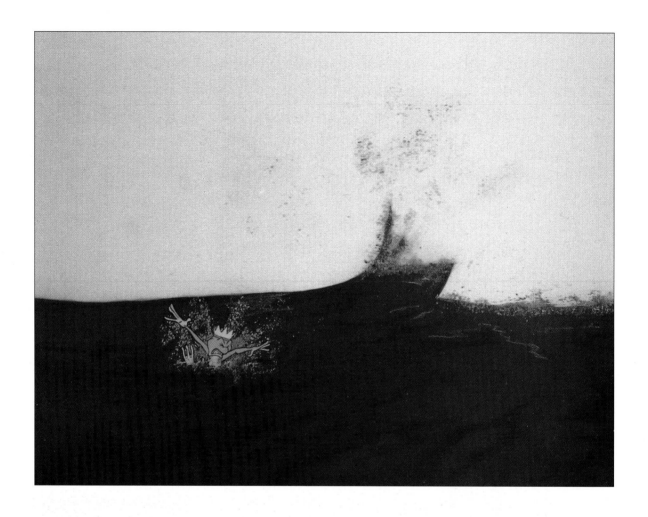

The little frog swam desperately down through the murky water, trying to avoid the hideous fate that Messina the snake had in store for him. Frederic twisted and turned, ducked and weaved, surfaced gasping, and dived again. Still the snake pursued him, lashing the water into a billowing storm in her rage. Then, exhausted and battered, and almost ready to admit defeat, Frederic seemed for a moment to see his father in the underwater reeds, and to hear his beloved voice encouraging him.

"Swim, Frederic, fear not, swim like a prince!" his father seemed to say, and Frederic suddenly found new strength to swim on towards the open sea. Messina had not won yet!

Frederic's courage had returned with his strength, and he swam on through the waters, with new hope in his heart. Even so, it seemed to him that he had been swimming for hours, with the murderous Messina still behind him. Frederic needed to find a hiding place, where perhaps he could work out a plan of escape while he rested. But where could he hide? The sea seemed to offer no help at all. Then Frederic noticed a dark hole in some rocks. The hole looked as though it stretched back into a cave. Perhaps, if he could get inside the cave before Messina spotted his escape, he could hide there for a time.

Frederic managed a burst of speed, and with a quick glance over his shoulder, he darted towards the hole, and wriggled inside. At last he could hide from Messina!

But just then, a stream of bubbles began to rise from the hole and floated past him, out into the sea. Messina, attracted by the bubbles, sped towards the hole – and towards Frederic. Now she had seen him, and Frederic was trapped! He cowered back in fear, thinking all was lost.

But just as Messina reached the hole and struck out at Frederic, a huge set of teeth snapped together over Frederic, enclosing him safely, and missing Messina by a bubble's width. The little frog-prince had been saved from Messina – but what had saved him? Was it something even worse?

Luckily for Frederic, he had been rescued by Nessie, the famous monster from Loch Ness, in Scotland. Nessie herself had been on

a trip to the North Sea, and had been resting behind a rock when Frederic had mistaken her gigantic mouth for a cave. He had swum right inside Nessie's mouth!

Not even Messina's evil magic had any effect against Nessie. And as long as Nessie was sheltering Frederic, Messina could not harm him, either.

When Messina came face to face with Nessie, she was furious! She had thought that the little frog-prince was hers to destroy, and now he had been snatched away at the moment of her victory. She lashed up a vicious tornado of rocks and water that whirled through the ocean in a storm of rage. But Frederic remained safe, and at last Messina gave up.

Then, from the very eye of the tornado, Messina shrieked a final message to Frederic. "You ugly little frog! One day I will catch up with you and destroy you, just as I destroyed your father – and your mother! Then I shall be all-powerful! I shall rule the world!"

And Messina returned to the castle, to plot her terrible revenge on Frederic, and to perfect her evil skills.

The wake of Messina's tornado had disturbed an enormous rock, which fell on Nessie's tail and trapped it against a reef. As Nessie grunted with pain and surprise, her cavernous mouth opened, and Frederic swam out once more. He was free again, and safe – at least for a time – from the dreadful Messina. But now what would happen?

As the little frog-prince turned to face the monstrous creature who had saved his life, he saw that her huge mouth, whose deadly sharp teeth had saved him from the dreaded Messina, was now curved into a gentle smile. Her kindly smiling eyes, looking into his, calmed his fears.

"Hello, little frog," said Nessie in her surprisingly high, sweet voice. "Don't be afraid; I won't hurt you."

And Frederic realised, with a rush of relief, that Nessie could be trusted. At last he had made a friend!

Frederic and Nessie spent hours talking. When Frederic explained that he was really a prince, and not a frog at all, Nessie tried to accept her friend's story. But she couldn't accept his name!

"My name is Frederic – Frederic the Great!" said Frederic, rather boastfully. Nessie decided to call him Freddie, and somehow the name seemed better for the frog that Prince Frederic had become.

When Nessie discovered that she couldn't move her tail, Freddie offered to help. At first, Nessie laughed to think that a tiny frog could help to move a gigantic rock – but she didn't know that

Freddie still had magic powers, even as a frog. With an enormous effort, Freddie managed to raise the rock, and free Nessie's tail. Then, after he'd rested, Nessie gave him a lift to the surface of the sea, and set him on his way beneath the night sky.

"I have to get back to Scotland," she explained. "But if you ever need any help, my dear, just whistle – like this!"

And as the sound of her whistled "*Ness – ie!*" echoed across the waves, Freddie sprang off, on his journey into the unknown.

2

FREDDIE IN FROGLAND

One thing was clear to Freddie now – he couldn't go back home to the castle! But where should he go, and what should he do with his life? Freddie felt confused by what had happened to him, and even more confused when he tried to imagine his future.

"Very well," he thought to himself, at last. "I've been turned into a frog, so a frog I will be! I'll forget all about being a prince, and learn froggy ways instead."

Before long, Freddie made his way to Frogland where he made friends with all the other frogs and joined in all their fun and games. There were endless parties, where Freddie learned to dance, and play in the band.

In winter, the frogs built snowfrogs on the icy slopes, skied, and skated all day on the pond. Then in spring, when the snow and ice had melted, the frogs had sliding competitions, and tumbled down the slopes into the warm, refreshing water.

But after a while, Freddie stopped enjoying the Frogland life so much. He found himself sitting apart from the other frogs, instead of joining in the games. And he began to wonder if he could still use any of his old magic powers . . .

The rock that Freddie picked for his magic experiment was large and heavy, and Freddie stared at it as hard as he could, concentrating all his efforts. At first, nothing happened – and then, slowly, the rock began to glow. Then, to Freddie's silent command, the rock rose in the air, and floated towards him. It paused, began to crack, and then, without a sound, exploded into millions of pieces!

The other frogs were amazed. "What power! What magic! What an extraordinary frog you are, Freddie," they croaked in an admiring chorus.

As time passed, Freddie realised that he could not stay in Frogland for ever: he did not really belong there.

Although he had almost forgotten his life as a prince, it was not just his magic powers that set him apart from the other frogs.

Freddie was growing bigger.

And bigger, and bigger, and bigger . . .

In fact, Freddie grew to such a size that he knew he was not a frog – or at least, not an ordinary one. And all the other frogs admitted it, too.

Now that Freddie had grown to be a man – or at the very least, a man-frog – he needed new clothes to go with his new personality. And once the frogs had provided these, it was time for him to go.

"I'll never forget you," he said fondly to all his friends. "You've helped me so much, but now I must go out into the world, and seek my fortune. I must use my magic powers to do good, and I must look for ways to help anyone who needs me."

So Freddie went off into the world, to fight evil, wherever evil was to be found.

3

THE MYSTERY OF THE DISAPPEARING MONUMENTS

M any years passed. Freddie settled in Paris and became a secret agent working for the French Secret Service. Freddie was a very special sort of secret agent indeed, for he used only his secret, magical powers and his cleverness in the fight against spies and criminals. He never carried weapons. And his only helper was a custom-made Frogmobile with a mind of her own: Freddie's trusted friend, Nicole.

Freddie's fame spread throughout France, and soon other countries had heard of the strange man-frog, secret agent FR07.

It was said he could solve any mystery, so when London's MI5 were baffled by a series of frightening crimes, they wasted no time in contacting him.

The telephone rang in Freddie's penthouse, high above Paris. "FR07? This is MI5, the British Secret Service, calling from London," said the voice at the other end. And, as Freddie listened, the Brigadier in charge of MI5 explained to Freddie what the problem was, and why they needed his help.

"All of Britain's most famous monuments are just disappearing into thin air," the Brigadier explained. "We have no idea who could be responsible!"

But a faint memory from the distant past nagged at the back of Freddie's mind. Perhaps he could think of someone powerful enough, and wicked enough, to attempt such a thing . . .

"Yes, yes," he replied. "I will come to London at once!"

The whole of London was in an uproar. One by one, and in the most mysterious way, the famous monuments were simply vanishing. One moment they were there – and the next, as if by magic, they were, quite simply, not there at all!

The first thing to go was Nelson's Column, from its home in Trafalgar Square. The tour guide who first reported it as missing could hardly believe it herself. The Column had been there – well, of course it had been there – when she had led her tour party into Trafalgar Square. She had taken the party across the pavement between the pigeons, and had first pointed out the National Gallery, on their right. But then, when everyone had turned to the left to look up at Nelson's Column, Nelson's Column had – well – just – gone!

20

The same thing happened to the
Tower of London. The world–famous
ravens who lived in the Tower
flapped and shrieked their surprise.
The Tower wasn't there, where they'd left
it that morning! All they'd done was fly around their favourite
visiting spots – up the river to Lambeth Palace, across to the
Houses of Parliament, and then back down the river to the Tower
in time for an afternoon nap.

And while they were away, the Tower had simply gone! There
was nowhere for them to land, and nowhere to roost! They were
homeless. And the ravens huddled together on the ground,
shocked and miserable.

21

The next building to disappear was Buckingham Palace! That very afternoon, the Queen returned from a tour abroad, and her carriage had just turned into the Mall to begin the drive down to the Palace.

"Home at last," said the TV commentator, speaking to the camera as the carriage approached the Palace. "Though Buckingham Palace is a palace to the rest of us, to Her Majesty it is simply home. . . " The commentator stopped dead, as he saw a strange beam of light descend from the sky. Then Buckingham Palace tilted slightly, and lifted majestically up into the air, along the beam of light! Then it disappeared.

Pandemonium broke out among the crowd, and the royal horses reared in the air in astonishment. The coachman bent down to the window. "Erm . . . Your Majesty, I don't know how to tell you this, but . . . Buckingham Palace seems to have gone."

"Gone? Gone? Where has it gone?" replied the Queen.

The coachman thought for a moment, and looked around.

"I dunno. The aliens must have got it . . ." he answered.

At MI5 headquarters that evening, the Brigadier tried to convince the Prime Minister that he had everything under control, with a really good plan of attack to solve the mysterious crimes. But the truth of the matter was, MI5 were baffled. At first the Brigadier had no idea what to do, or where to begin. All his best secret agents had gone missing in other parts of the world, and the Brigadier had no one left in MI5 whom he could rely on in this crisis. He was surrounded by office men, he thought gloomily to himself: good at pushing pencils around, but not much use at dealing with criminals. What he really needed was a leader: a resourceful, intelligent and courageous agent, ready to deal with the unexpected. And there was no one!

At least, there was no one British to rely on, but there was just one secret agent who might be able to help . . .

Trilby, one of the Brigadier's assistants, stood by an enormous map of Britain, on which he had stuck various pegs. Each of the pegs was the same shape as the vanished building which it represented. The number of pegs on the map was growing steadily.

Trilby selected two more pegs from his box: one for Stonehenge, and one for St Paul's Cathedral.

"I wonder what's going to be next?" Trilby asked the meeting, innocently.

Just then the radio sprang into life. "Stonehenge is missing! Stonehenge is missing! And St Paul's is missing! St Paul's is missing!"

The meeting groaned in dismay, but Trilby gave a small smile as he pressed the pegs he had already chosen into place on the map. Then he turned to the Brigadier.

"I thought you said you had a plan, sir?" he said, smoothly.

"Yes. Only one hope remains now. I've asked the French Secret Service to send me over their top man. In fact, he's on his way right now." The Brigadier's voice began to sound more cheerful as he remembered the telephone conversation he'd had earlier. "This agent is the best in the world. He's solved the most difficult and dangerous mysteries, and he's dealt with the most wicked of spies. He's none other than FR07!"

24

But when Freddie entered the room, there was an awkward silence. Everyone stood with their jaws dropped and their eyes wide with surprise. They were startled to see that FR07 was, in fact, a frog! Even the Brigadier was shocked out of his usual good manners for a moment, although only Trilby was rude enough to laugh out loud.

Freddie's eyes twinkled in amusement at the reaction he received, but he lost no time in putting everyone at their ease. He introduced himself to the Brigadier, and reminded him of their telephone conversation.

The Brigadier quickly recovered himself, and brought Freddie up to date about the most recent disappearances. Then, full of enthusiasm, and throwing a friendly arm around Freddie's shoulders, he led him towards the door.

"I can guarantee you the backing of all our facilities. Scientific gadgets, for instance – you name 'em, we've got 'em," the Brigadier promised. "Let me show you around."

As they reached the operational
wing of the building, they entered a
room where a young woman,
dressed ready for action in a martial
arts outfit, was practising tai chi. A flying
object immediately began to buzz around the
Brigadier's head, and he brushed it away
impatiently.

"That's a flying bug – de-activate it
please, Daffers!"

And then he introduced Freddie to
the young woman, "Daffers" – Daphne Fortescue-Fortescue, one
of MI5's leading technical scientists. All her inventions were at
Freddie's disposal.

Freddie sensed that he could trust Daffers and he liked her
immediately, but he explained that he didn't use gadgets of any
kind in his work.

"Then what about weapons?" asked the Brigadier, and led
Freddie on through the building to the weapons section, where he
introduced a small, dark-haired man. "This is Scotty McGunn, Head
of Weapons. He can get you anything: guns, rockets, lasers . . . "
And Scotty whipped open his coat, to reveal a fierce array of
weapons hanging on either side.

But although Freddie warmed to
the quiet Scotsman, he shook his
head. "The only weapons I ever
use are my thoughts," he
said softly. "The powers
of the mind
will always
overcome
violence."

Just then, one of the television screens in the background flickered into life, and a newscaster appeared.

"This is the BBC, and here is a news flash. Canterbury Cathedral has disappeared! Canterbury Cathedral has disappeared!"

The telephone rang. It was the Prime Minister asking the Brigadier what he was going to do. Desperately, the Brigadier turned to Freddie, still clutching the phone.

"Will you take the job?" he asked.

Freddie smiled as he glanced around the room. "How can I refuse?" he asked.

The Brigadier was delighted – and had a sudden idea. Why didn't Freddie take Daffers and Scotty to help him?

Freddie usually worked alone, but when he saw their eager faces, he changed his mind. Perhaps this time it would be useful to have colleagues with him.

Daffers and Scotty were eager to begin work, but even they were startled when Freddie suggested starting at the Ascot races! Trilby couldn't conceal a sneer at the news. Ascot! How absurd. Trust a foreigner to start off on the wrong foot . . . and Trilby hurried off to a mysterious meeting, while Freddie, Daffers and Scotty left to get ready for the races: Daffers and Scotty with mixed feelings, and Freddie with his feelings kept to himself.

The Brigadier was left trying to explain to the Prime Minister that the mission to find the missing buildings lay in capable hands.

THE RACE BEGINS

Now dressed in their best clothes and seated in Nicole – the Frogmobile – Freddie, Daffers and Scotty set off for Ascot. Nicole was well behaved as long as they were in fast city traffic, but as soon as they reached the country roads and a traffic jam, the Frogmobile grew impatient.

"Now, behave yourself, Nicole," said Freddie.

But Nicole had had enough of the quiet life! She gently hopped on to the roof of the car in front, and then sprang her way carefully along the line of traffic. All went well until Nicole failed to notice an open-top car in front – and she landed squarely on the heads of the people inside!

There was no time to apologise! Nicole whizzed off in embarrassment and at great speed, and in no time at all they had reached Ascot.

Now, Freddie outlined his idea to Daffers and Scotty. Clearly, they were up against a massive organisation, with spies all over the country. And the only way to smoke spies out of the woodpile, said Freddie, was to make yourself a sitting target. They should show themselves, and wait for the enemy to move first.

Freddie did not have long to wait. Four men in the crowd had watched them arrive, and tailed Freddie as he placed a bet. Then, as Freddie strolled along the terraces, the four men suddenly appeared around him.

"We have a message for you, FR07," hissed their leader. "And the message is . . . death!"

And all four men launched themselves at Freddie.

But Freddie was more than a match for them, and his super-agility, strength and daring soon made short work of the four men.

Then, as they lay gasping on the ground, Freddie made a gigantic leap into the air. *Voilà,* he landed safely on the very top level of the terraces. There, he could overhear the men's conversation without being seen by them. "He's escaped!" groaned the leader, when he could speak again. "We must report to El Supremo!" As the leader took out a walkie-talkie, Freddie leaned forward.

Far away, behind his snake-like desk, El Supremo took the call. He was furious! "Fools! Imbeciles! You weren't supposed to kill FR07, only follow and observe him. Now that you have failed in that, return at once and prepare for tonight's attack, on Big Ben!"

31

As Freddie had guessed, he was up against his old enemy, the dreaded Messina. In a vast underground complex she and her henchman, El Supremo, had assembled the world's most feared dictators, generals and master criminals. Their headquarters were packed with the latest technology and scientific gadgets. And, as the snake she had become, Messina ruled over it all!

Her evil song hypnotised everyone unlucky enough to enter Messina's terrible presence, so that they, too, fell under the Power of the Snake. Like a vision of destruction, Messina's hissing song struck terror into the hearts of even the most heartless of her allies.

"With a mission to destroy
 Take you, shake you, break you
 Till it's time
 For me to take control.
 The poison's in your very soul
 You're bound to fall;
 I'll win it all –
 Your world is mine!
 Yes! I'm the Queen!"

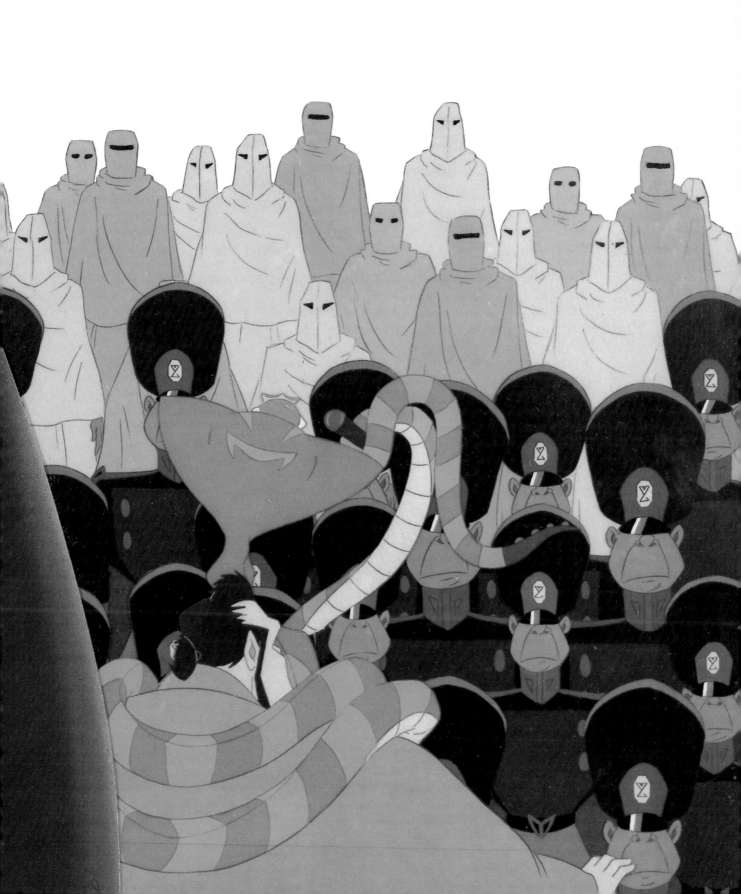

5

THE RACE CONTINUES

That evening, all the power of the British Army, Navy and Air Force, as well as the police, was assembled to encircle Windsor Castle – just as Freddie had hoped. He had told Daffers and Scotty that Windsor Castle was the next target, and had kept his discovery that it was really Big Ben to himself.

The Brigadier had the sticky task of explaining to the Queen, who had taken refuge in Windsor Castle, that she had to move once again. The news was not welcomed!

"I'm terribly sorry, Your Majesty," said the Brigadier helplessly, as Trilby watched, smirking. But the Queen's car roared away. "I was only going to say that I do . . . have . . . a plan," gasped the Brigadier, running after it.

Meanwhile, unknown to the Brigadier, the Frogmobile had dropped Freddie, Daffers and Scotty at Big Ben. Once they were inside and had climbed up to the clock room, Freddie explained to his startled companions that Big Ben was the true target of attack that night, and not Windsor Castle at all. Daffers and Scotty were speechless with confusion. Why on earth had Freddie lied to them?

"It was necessary to distract the Brigadier," he explained. "The Brigadier is a soldier, and he wants to capture the enemy. But that is not enough! We must penetrate the enemy headquarters, and the only way to achieve that is to let them capture us."

Daffers and Scotty were not convinced, but there was nothing they could do. Freddie had removed the batteries from Daffer's walkie-talkie, and so her efforts to contact the Brigadier were useless. They were completely cut off from the outside world. Now, they could only wait.

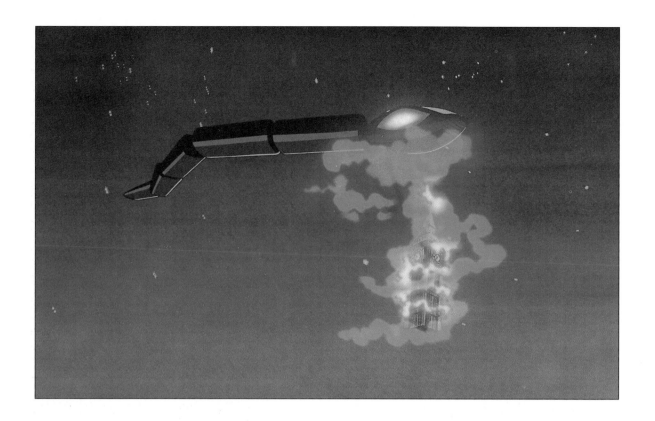

Overhead, a sinister space ship, in the shape of a giant snake, slithered menacingly towards Big Ben. Then a beam of light shot from its head, and the clock tower began to shake.

Inside the tower, Daffers and Scotty had to stop themselves from falling, while Freddie balanced easily, as calm as ever.

The beam of light wrapped itself sinuously around Big Ben and the whole tower lifted towards the snake ship. In horror, Scotty pulled a gun from his coat, but Freddie laughed at him.

"Who are you going to shoot, Scotty? Put it away! Enjoy the flight!"

Daffers used her pocket electronic compass to track their direction, as the snake ship drew Big Ben away from London. They seemed to be going north.

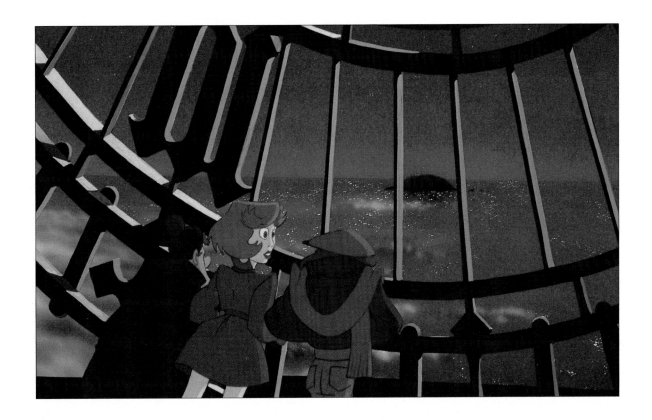

After a while, Daffers checked again. "We're heading for a small island off the east coast of Scotland," she said. "It's called the Isle of Worms!"

"But I know that island," said Scotty, slowly. "It's uninhabited, except for the creepy-crawlies that live there!" As they peered out of the clock face they saw that Scotty was right: the island was just a small, barren rock. But as the snake ship hovered above the island, the ground suddenly parted in the middle, like a giant mouth. A tunnel stretched behind the mouth, into darkness. The snake ship descended into the tunnel taking Big Ben with it. Then the huge mouth closed again, and all was quiet.

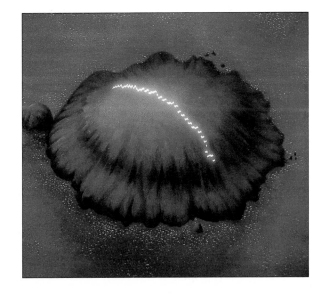

6

THE ISLE OF WORMS

T he sensors on the Isle of Worms had picked up Daffers, Scotty and Freddie as soon as Big Ben arrived, and so El Supremo and Messina were ready and waiting for their guests. They were greeted with fiendish glee.

"Welcome to our little nest," gloated El Supremo, while Messina the snake curled sinuously around his shoulders.

While Daffers and Scotty recovered their nerve, Freddie joked with El Supremo and Messina. He seemed to be unconcerned with his predicament – but anyone who knew him well would have realised that Freddie was at his most dangerous when he seemed to be laughing and joking. Luckily, El Supremo and

Messina were no match for
his deception!

El Supremo couldn't resist
showing off, to try to
impress the famous Freddie.

"Let me demonstrate what
I can do to your beloved Big
Ben," he crowed. "Behold
the Power of the Snake!"

And picking up a
diminishing machine, El Supremo pulled down a lever at the side.
A ray of light hit Big Ben. Then, as the ray intensified, Big Ben
silently and swiftly shrank, to the size of a small model!

Freddie and his companions could not conceal their horror,
and El Supremo and Messina chuckled in glee – while Freddie
secretly noted the position of the diminishing machine on the
command desk.

El Supremo couldn't resist continuing the show. Why not, after
all? The three intruders could be safely dealt with later by Messina
and the guards, and meantime, he had a ready-made audience to
react to his revelations. He might as well enjoy their horrified
amazement for a while longer.

"And now, my friends," he laughed, "let me show you my little
collection of treasures!"

A lift took everyone down into a huge chamber further
underground, which pulsated with a strange, multi-coloured light.
And there, in the centre of the treasure chamber, were all the
stolen buildings – all now shrunk to the size of models, and
grouped around a strange box. As they watched, the three friends
saw that a sort of misty, ghost-like light was passing from the
buildings into the box in the middle. Freddie's eyes narrowed as
he suddenly began to realise what was happening, and Daffers
and Scotty gasped in horror.

When the miniature Big Ben was added to the collection, El Supremo swept his arm to indicate the scene.

"Here is the history of your country," he said. "The culture, the backbone of Britain. For centuries your people have loved them, fought for them, died for them. And my little box can extract the energies which lie dormant within the stone, and turn it from positive, to negative!

"All the life force of your history will be gone. Your people will become dull and sleepy, and finally your whole country will be at a standstill! And then . . ."

El Supremo flicked a switch, and a giant video screen flickered to life. It showed a host of submarines, lurking in the depths of the North Sea beyond the Isle of Worms, and ready to be launched against Britain.

"Invasion, defeat and slavery will follow!" shouted El Supremo in glee. Then he turned to Freddie, with a triumphant laugh. "Now you see, FR07, the true Power of the Snake!"

The three friends, their guards, and El Supremo returned to the command room, as El Supremo finished his terrible explanation.

"I need only one more piece in my little jigsaw," he murmured. "Then, FR07, the conquest of Britain will begin! And after Britain – the world!"

And as they re-entered the control room, the last building that El Supremo needed to complete his preparations arrived. Scotty was horror-struck.

"Oh, no!" he gasped. "It's Edinburgh Castle!"

Now, nothing stood between El Supremo and the realisation of his dreams, except Freddie and his companions. With fiendish delight, El Supremo settled down to watch Messina destroy them!

At first, it seemed as though her task would be easy, for Scotty – her first target – was no match for her. But just as she had started to crush him in her coils, Freddie escaped from his guards and, with a mighty and daring leap, landed on the snake! Scotty rolled away, safe for the moment, whilst Freddie began a life-or-death battle with his old enemy.

As they fought, El Supremo opened a hatch in the floor, leading to a whirlpool in which hungry sea monsters lurked. As Messina and Freddie rolled towards it, it seemed as though Freddie was losing. But suddenly, Freddie straightened his powerful frog's legs,

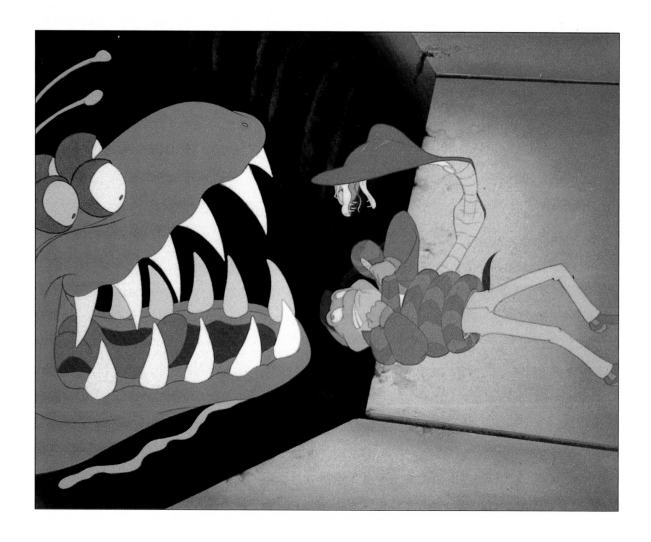

and with an enormous effort shot Messina off into the air! She landed wrapped around a pole, hissing in fury and badly winded. Freddie had won – at least for the moment!

But Freddie's triumph could not last long, for the odds were stacked heavily against him. As he turned, he saw Daffers and Scotty standing with the guards' laser guns trained at their heads. With his companions in such danger, there could be no easy escape for any of them. And now, El Supremo made his plans to dispose of all three companions. He decided that Daffers would stay at headquarters, so that she could be indoctrinated in the Power of the Snake. Freddie and Scotty had an even worse fate in front of them, for El Supremo's dreadful decision for them involved the sea of monsters, in the depths of the North Sea.

El Supremo shouted his orders, and a huge steel cage descended from the ceiling. It fell neatly into place over Freddie and Scotty, and locked on to a section of the metal floor. Then as Daffers watched helplessly, a huge hook lifted the cage, and swung it into the hatch in the floor. The cage sank into the water, and the floor slid silently back into place over the hatch. And as Daffers was dragged off by the guards, El Supremo turned to Messina in triumph.

"We have nothing to fear, my Queen. No one can stop us now. The Power of the Snake has defeated FR07!"

Now that the energies had been extracted from the stolen buildings, the Power of the Snake could be used to put Britain to sleep, so that the invasion could take place.

The powerful rays shone out all over the country. And now, there were no defences.

All over the land, slowly but surely, people grew tired. They yawned, dropped their heads, and fell asleep. Teachers stopped their lessons in the middle of sentences, and children stopped writing with their pencils in mid-air. The roads were sudddenly deserted, as all the drivers pulled over to the side, switched off their engines, and fell asleep at their wheels.

At Wembley Stadium, the football match slowed to a stop just as a goal was about to be kicked. And across London in the Royal Albert Hall, the whole orchestra, the conductor and the audience all fell into a deep sleep, just before the climax of the concert.

There seemed to be no defences at all against the Power of the Snake and the Maximum Ray. Was there no one left to save Britain? Would El Supremo triumph in his terrible plans to take over not only Britain, but the whole world?

45

7

NESSIE TO THE RESCUE

Deep under the water, Freddie and Scotty were trapped in their cage, while the hungry sea monsters circled closer and closer. Freddie, of course, was perfectly at ease in water, but poor Scotty gasped for air. He couldn't last much longer!

Freddie took a deep breath and blew air into Scotty's lungs with the kiss of life. Then, taking another deep breath, Freddie whistled two high-pitched notes through the murky waters. "*Ness-ie!*" And he settled down to wait.

The whistle travelled far through the water till it reached Nessie, in Loch Ness. And, immediately recognising her old friend's distress call, Nessie sped to his aid. The hungry monsters scattered like a shoal of minnows, and Nessie quickly prised open the bars of the cage, grasped Scotty in her tail, and shot to the surface. She was just in time to save him! When Freddie joined them Scotty was safe on a rock, coughing up water, but not much the worse for wear.

Freddie hurried off with Nessie, leaving Scotty on his rock. Passing El Supremo's submarines on the way, they soon arrived at Nessie's home, where all her family were gathered in welcome.

Then Nessie turned to her friend. "Now, what was it you were wanting, Freddie dear?" she asked.

"Just a little help from my friends," replied Freddie, smiling, and he quickly explained his plan, before Nessie and her family speedily swam off to put his idea into action.

If Freddie's plan was to succeed, every second counted. At that very moment, El Supremo was giving his final orders to the submarine commander, over the television monitor, as the submarines lay poised for action in the depths of the North Sea.

"Now, commander, now!" cried El Supremo. "Attack!"

And, as the screen went blank, Messina curled around to smile at El Supremo in triumph.

"Britain is finished," gloated El Supremo. "Now we can start on the rest of the world, my beauty!"

Then both of them turned to Daffers, who sat blank-faced

beside them at the control room desk. Messina the snake hissed once, in command, and Daffers responded instantly.

"The snake – shall rule – the world," murmured Daffers, as though hypnotised. "The snake – shall rule – the world!"

Messina hissed a command again, and Daffers stopped her mindless chanting instantly, as if a tap had been switched off.

El Supremo and Messina laughed with glee at their success – in fact, they laughed too much to notice Daffers's sudden change of expression, or her whisper of despair: "Oh Freddie, where are you?"

Just then, far out at sea, the submarine commander was in a fury of rage, for none of his submarines were moving.

"I said full steam ahead, you imbeciles!" he raged. But it was too late – Nessie and her companions had succeeded, just in time. Their strong seaweed ropes were safely tied around the submarines' propellers, and all the submarines were locked together in a helpless circle.

"Thanks, Nessie – see you later!" cried Freddie, and with that he swam off to rejoin Scotty.

Then, Freddie quickly explained the next part of his plan to Scotty, as they swam together towards the secret gate which Freddie had noticed, leading to the underground headquarters.

49

There, pretending to be unconscious, Freddie slumped in
Scotty's arms for just long enough to fool the guards. Then, when
the guards dashed up, Freddie's long legs caught them both with
unexpected blows on their chins, and knocked them senseless!

Freddie and Scotty then put on the guards' masks and tunics –
and well disguised, stepped boldly inside the enemy's doors.

8

FREDDIE THE SUPERHERO

F reddie's luck seemed to be holding, for almost immediately he and Scotty saw Daffers coming towards them, guarded by two of El Supremo's henchmen. As soon as they had passed, Freddie turned to surprise the guards, who fell helplessly to the floor, unconscious, at his touch.

Daffers was delighted to see them both alive and well. After quick explanations all round, Freddie and Scotty took over as Daffers's new "guards", and the three friends marched solemnly together, towards the treasure chamber. There, the guard demanded the password.

"The password is – *Freddie* shall rule the world!" cried Daffers happily, as the three of them launched their surprise attack.

There were more than twenty guards inside the treasure chamber, but the companions had courage, skill and determination on their side, and they made short work of the opposition: Freddie with his extraordinary super-leaps and kicks, Daffers with her remarkable tai chi, and Scotty with just one of his special weapons – a haggis-shaped baton! Soon, all the guards were slumped unconscious on the floor.

But as the last guard fell, he knocked the central box, which was still beaming forth the sleep rays into Britain. Now the rays were directed on Scotty and Daffers who began to stagger under the ray's irresistible effects!

"Help! Freddie, help us!" cried Daffers in despair, as she and Scotty slumped to the floor. Freddie realised that desperate measures were necessary. Fighting off the full impact of the rays with all his magic powers, Freddie battled his way towards the

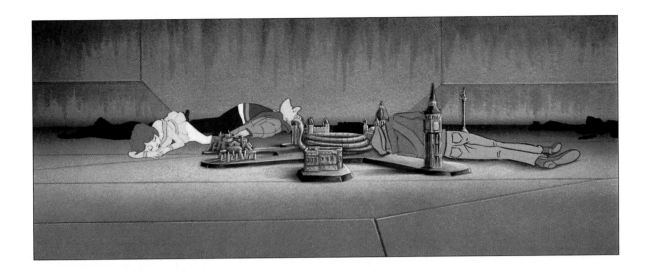

box. But even Freddie's super strength was taxed to the limit! Just managing to pick up the box and dash it to the ground, Freddie slumped down, exhausted, and fell unconscious!

The sleep box destroyed, people all over Britain began to wake up, and carry on as though nothing had happened. Teachers finished their sentences and children put their pencils back down

on to the paper in front of them; the footballer scored a goal at Wembley Stadium, and the orchestra finished playing its music in the Royal Albert Hall to roaring applause.

But as alarm bells rang and lights flashed in the control room, El Supremo checked his instruments, and hissed in rage and fear.

"The sleep ray has stopped! FR07 must have escaped and forced his way into my treasure chamber! I will kill him!"

In the treasure chamber, Daffers and Scotty slowly got back on their feet, but Freddie remained unconscious as El Supremo and the new guards rushed in. El Supremo raised his deadly laser sword over Freddie's body.

"You have tried to destroy my plan, FR07, but you will not succeed! Now, you die!"

Although he could not open his eyes, let alone move, Freddie was aware of what was happening to him. His mind flashed back to his childhood, and the day his father taught him about swords.

"Fear not the sword, my son," his father had said. "The true powers of the mind are greater than any weapon . . ."

And then, as Daffers screamed a warning, Freddie's eyes snapped open, just as El Supremo's sword began its vicious descent. Immediately, Freddie's strength returned, and the sword was halted in its path by his magical powers. Then, leaping to his feet, Freddie sent El Supremo himself sprawling to the floor!

And now yet another battle raged! Once again, Freddie's agility
and daring, combined with Daffers's and Scotty's special skills,
soon flattened all El Supremo's troops. Only the leader himself
was left standing before them. With one look of great contempt,
Freddie turned his back on the cruel and defeated leader, and
began to walk off with Daffers and Scotty.

But that was too much for El Supremo! With an enraged cry,
he rushed after the companions with his sword raised ready to
strike. Freddie's nimble leap took him out of danger, and enabled
him to trip up El Supremo as well, so that he crashed to the
ground once more.

But the desperate El Supremo had more tricks up his sleeve.
Suddenly, he ran to the collection of miniaturised buildings. Lifting
his sword, he made one last stand.

"Surrender, FR07, or I will destroy Big Ben!"

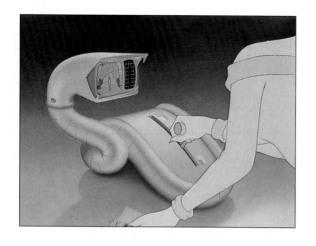

Freddie pretended to surrender, and began to walk slowly towards El Supremo – but behind his back, he signalled to Daffers to take the miniaturising machine from the desk, and reverse the switch.

Daffers quickly came to the rescue. She pushed the lever and Big Ben suddenly shot back up to full size – and El Supremo was caught on the hands of the clock and hauled into the air as well! Then, when they miniaturised Big Ben once more, El Supremo was shrunk to a miniature, too!

But there was one last danger to overcome. Messina the snake had been hiding on a chair, watching in dismay as her world, her power, and all her plans crumbled to dust. Now, with all her other chances gone, she struck out at Daffers. Freddie, realising how dangerous she was, decided that the others should stay out of this fight, and came to the rescue.

"This is a family affair," he explained grimly. "Stay back from her!" And then, he turned to the snake. "I'm not the little frog of long ago," he said. "I do not fear you now. Whatever ugly shape you take, I shall defeat you!"

Even with Freddie's powers, the fight was a dangerous one. First, Messina turned herself into a vampire bat, and flew straight for Freddie's throat – but Freddie jumped sideways, and the bat crashed into the wall behind him.

Then, sliding to the ground, the bat became an enormous, drooling hyena, and charged, baring her yellow fangs and growling horribly. But Freddie leaped nimbly into the air, and the hyena grabbed the leg of the desk, instead of Freddie.

Now the hyena disappeared, and for a few minutes, all was quiet. Had Messina gone for good?

"Behind you, Freddie!" cried Daffers, suddenly.

A scorpion had appeared, and struck at Freddie's feet, but he danced nimbly around her, just out of her reach, until she ran out of steam. Then Freddie tried to imprison the scorpion in a bowl, but just as he did so, the scorpion became a giant python, and, bursting through the bowl, coiled herself around Freddie's body. Slowly but surely, the coils tightened, and the air was squeezed out of Freddie's lungs.

As he struggled for breath, half-fainting, Freddie again remembered his father. And he seemed to hear his father's words, as Freddie had once joked about being out of breath. "Your strength, Frederic, will always be *beyond* your last breath," his father had said.

With an enormous burst of

strength, Freddie sprang back to consciousness, and began to unwrap the python's coils! When he had unravelled her, he swung her around his head, faster and faster! Messina shrieked in anger and fear, knowing she had lost the battle.

And then, at last, Freddie released her. Up she flew, high into the control room, unable to stop herself, and smashed against the girders in the roof. She hung there, hurt. And then, as the companions watched breathlessly, Messina managed one last, slow and painful change. The python turned into a vulture – with a wounded, dangling wing.

As she flew off, flapping awkwardly in defeat, Messina's exhausted voice echoed back to the watchers.

"One day . . . one day you will pay for this . . ."

Now the Brigadier arrived, and was lowered into the control room by helicopter – just missing the Messina-vulture.

Daffers and Scotty had a lot to explain, and to show the Brigadier. Together with Freddie, they made a special trip back to the treasure chamber. There, they were able to show him that all the stolen buildings were safe, and could be returned to their rightful places and made full size once more. The tiny figure of El Supremo still hung foolishly from the hands of Big Ben, no longer able to menace the world with his evil.

Freddie reached over, picked up El Supremo by the scruff of his neck, and dropped him neatly into a matchbox.

"There you are, sir," he said, giving the box to the Brigadier. "And now it's time we went home: we have one more little job to do there."

9

A HERO'S WELCOME

B ack at MI5, Freddie was in time to see Trilby being arrested as a traitor.

"But Freddie," asked the Brigadier in amazement, "how did you know that Trilby was a spy for El Supremo?"

Freddie explained that he had noticed the snake tattoo on Trilby's wrist, as well as his strange behaviour.

Then, while the others were talking, Freddie slipped away, back to Nicole who was parked all by herself.

"I'm sorry, Nicole," said Freddie as he was reunited with his sulking friend. "I've been neglecting you, I know."

There were still some things left to do. All the buildings had to be returned to their rightful places – and it was a lot easier to do that while they were still miniature-sized.

The Queen was allowed to make Buckingham Palace the right size herself. First, the tiny Buckingham Palace was put carefully into place, in exactly the right position. Then Freddie explained to Her Majesty how to reverse the switch on the miniaturising machine. And then, everyone cheered as Buckingham Palace returned to the right size once more!

There was a champagne party at MI5, before Freddie left for Paris. The Brigadier explained to Freddie that because everyone was so impressed with his work, the world leaders wanted him to be a sort of Global Trouble-shooter, and sort out the problems of the world.

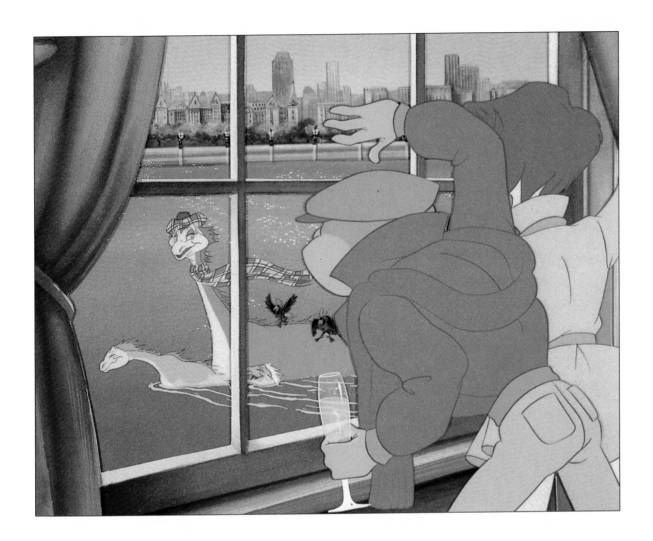

"So, what do you say, Freddie?" asked the Brigadier anxiously, while Daffers and Scotty held their breath in hope. Freddie hesitated for only a moment.

"Well," he replied slowly, "it might be possible. But only on one condition . . . can I take my two brilliant assistants with me?"

Just then, Daffers glanced out of the window.

"Freddie, look! You seem to have another fan club out there!"

And, as everyone watched, Nessie and all her friends and relations swam up the Thames, and waved joyously to Freddie. His happiness was complete!

The Freddie Library

Have you read all the Freddie books? These are the titles:

FREDDIE AS FR07
PRINCE FREDERIC   THE ISLE OF WORMS
FREDDIE GOES TO LONDON   FREDDIE SAVES THE DAY